The Little Mermaid

Series Editor: Sorrel Pitts
Text adapted by Coleen Degnan-Veness
Illustrated by Milly Teggle

LADYBIRD BOOKS

UK | USA | Canada | Ireland | Australia
India | New Zealand | South Africa

Ladybird Books is part of the Penguin Random House group of companies
whose addresses can be found at global.penguinrandomhouse.com.
www.penguin.co.uk www.puffin.co.uk www.ladybird.co.uk

First published 2017
001

Printed in China

A CIP catalogue record for this book is available from the British Library

ISBN: 978-0-241-29874-9

All correspondence to
Ladybird Books
Penguin Random House Children's
80 Strand, London WC2R 0RL

The Little Mermaid

Picture words

mermaid

tail

land

ship

prince

storm

palace

princess

There was a little mermaid who lived under the ocean with her father and her sisters. Like all mermaids, she had a beautiful tail, and she could sing very well.

The little mermaid's sisters were older. They could swim above the water, where they could see the land. But the little mermaid was too young to swim there.

The little mermaid's sisters told her about people who lived on the land. These people walked on two legs! The little mermaid wanted to see the people, too.

A few years later, the little mermaid swam above the water for the first time.

She saw a ship, and on the ship there was a young prince with a lovely face. When she saw him, she knew that she loved him.

Suddenly, a terrible storm came across the ocean, with strong winds and lots of rain. The ship turned in the water, and the prince fell in. His leg was hurt, and he could not swim.

"I have to help him!"
said the little mermaid.

The little mermaid took the prince to the land, and she stayed with him until the storm stopped.

When the prince opened his eyes, he saw the little mermaid looking down at him.

Then, the little mermaid saw people who were coming to help the prince, so she swam away.

When the little mermaid arrived back home, she told her sisters that she loved the young prince.

One of her sisters knew where the prince lived.

"I can take you there," she said.

The little mermaid swam with her sister to the prince's palace. There, she saw the prince walking near the ocean. She watched him for a long time.

After that, the little mermaid swam back to watch the prince again and again.

She knew that people did not love mermaids. And she knew that she could not live on the land with her tail.

The little mermaid wanted to be a person so that she could be with the prince.

The little mermaid felt very sad.

Her sisters said, "Go to the magic woman of the ocean. She can help."

The little mermaid went to the magic woman. "I love a prince," she told her. "Can you change me into a person, so that I can be with him on the land?"

"I have a magic drink that will change your tail into legs," said the magic woman of the ocean. "But if you drink it, you will not speak until the prince loves you. Do you want the drink?"

"Yes," said the little mermaid.

"After you drink this, you will go to sleep," said the magic woman of the ocean. "When you wake up, you will not have your tail. You will have two legs."

The little mermaid swam to the prince's palace. She drank the magic drink, and soon she was asleep.

When she woke up, she did not have her tail. She had two legs!

Soon, the prince walked down to the ocean, and he saw the little mermaid.

“You look like the girl who saved me in a storm,” he said. “Are you that girl?”

The little mermaid did not answer, because she could not speak!

"Come with me," said the prince. "You can stay in my palace. I want to know who you are. Can't you speak?"

But the little mermaid could not answer, and she could not tell him that she loved him.

One day, a beautiful princess came to the palace.

The little mermaid watched the prince while he was walking with the princess. They were talking, and the prince looked happy.

The little mermaid felt very sad.

"My father wants me to marry the princess," the prince told the little mermaid. "But I want to marry the girl who saved me in the storm."

The prince went for a walk by the ocean. The little mermaid followed him.

When the prince turned and looked into the little mermaid's eyes, he understood. She loved him.

Then, he knew who she was!

"You are the girl who saved me!" said the prince. "You are the girl that I love! Will you be my wife?"

"Yes, I will!" said the little mermaid.

The prince loved her — so now she could speak again.

The little mermaid and the prince got married. They were very happy with their new life together.

The little mermaid saw her sisters in the ocean waving to her. They were very happy because the little mermaid was with her young prince.

Activities

The key below describes the skills practiced in each activity.

 Spelling and writing

 Reading

 Speaking

 Critical thinking

 Preparation for the Cambridge Young Learners Exams

1 Match the words to the pictures.

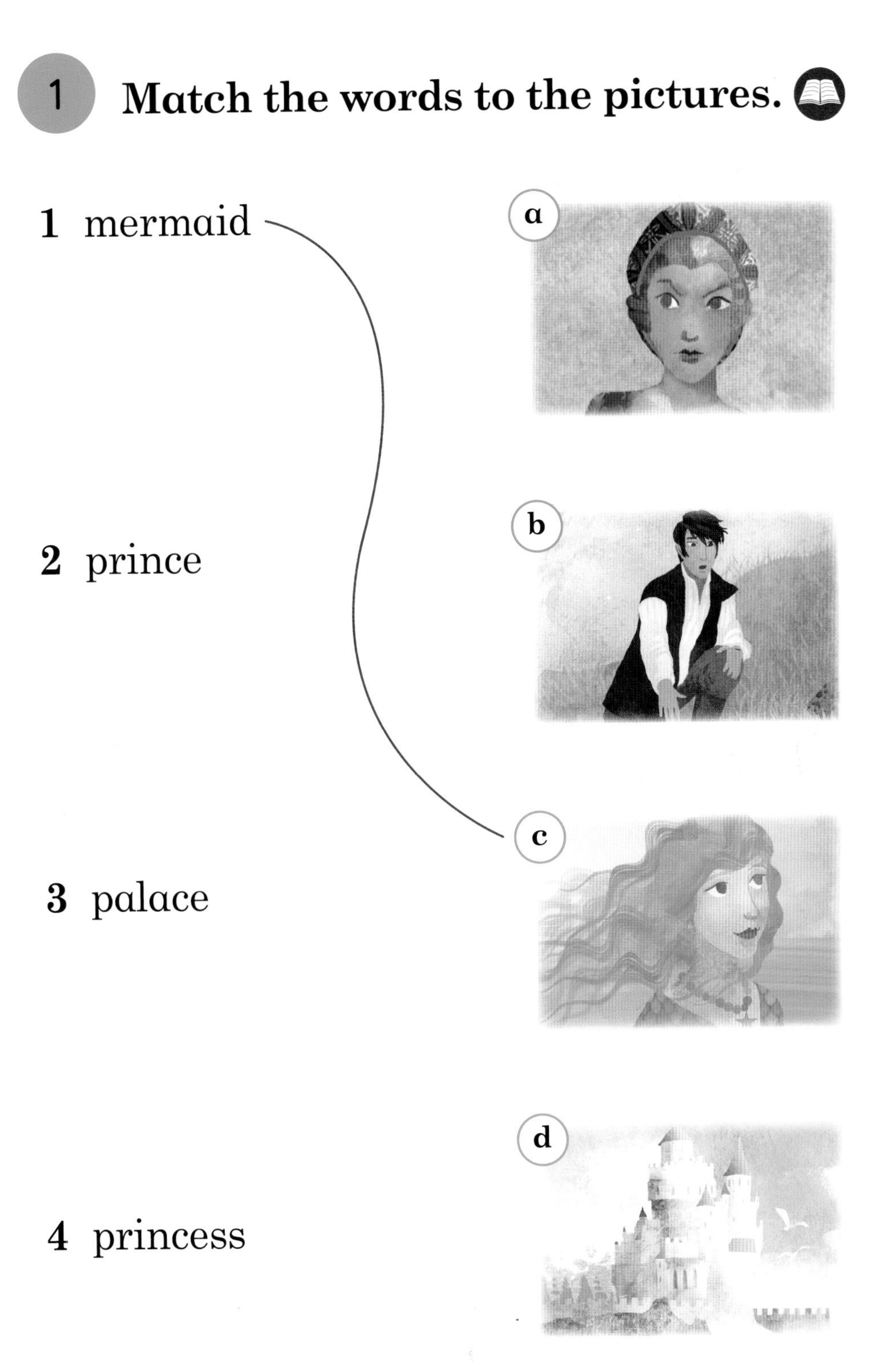

2 Look and read.

Write *yes* or *no*.

There was a little mermaid who
lived under the ocean with her
father and her sisters. Like all
mermaids, she had a beautiful
tail, and she could sing very well.

1 The little mermaid lived with her father and sisters. ......yes......

2 Her family lived under the ocean. ....

3 The little mermaid and her sisters had arms and legs. ....

4 The little mermaid and her sisters had beautiful tails. ....

5 The little mermaid could not sing very well. ....

3 Look and read. Choose the correct words and write them on the lines.

mermaid palace princess prince

1 In stories, this is half girl and half fish. mermaid

2 The daughter of a king. ....

3 The son of a king. ....

4 Where a king and his family live. ....

4 Circle the incorrect words. Write the correct words on the lines.

1 The little mermaid's sisters were younger than her. older

2 The sisters could see mermaids on the land. ....

3 The little mermaid couldn't swim above the water, because she was too old. ....

4 The sisters told the little mermaid about people who swam on two legs. ....

5 Look at the letters. Write the words.

1 a m s w

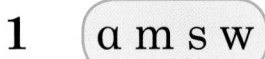

A few years later, the little mermaid ......swam...... above the water for the first time.

2 n p r c e i

She saw a young .... with a lovely face.

3 l e s g

He had long, brown hair and two ....

4 l d o e v

When she saw him, she knew that she .... him.

6 Look and read. Put a ✓ or a X in the boxes.

Suddenly, a terrible storm came across the ocean, with strong winds and lots of rain. The ship turned in the water, and the prince fell in. His leg was hurt, and he could not swim.
"I have to help him!" said the little mermaid.
12
13

1 A terrible storm came across the land. 

2 It brought soft winds and a bit of rain. ☐

3 The prince hurt his leg when he fell from the ship. ☐

4 The prince could swim. ☐

5 The little mermaid called for help. ☐

7 **Read the text. Choose the correct words and write them next to 1—5.**

storm mermaid prince ship land

A terrible [1] ....storm.... came across the ocean. The [2] .... turned in the water. The [3] .... fell in and hurt his leg. Now, he could not swim. The little [4] .... said, "I have to help him!" She swam to the prince, and took him to the [5] .... She stayed with him until the storm stopped.

8 Work with a friend. Talk about the two pictures. How are they different?

In picture a, the sky is blue.

In picture b, there is a storm.

9 Choose the correct answers.

1 Who was the little mermaid looking at?

a the other people **b** the prince

2 What did the prince see when he opened his eyes?

a the ship **b** the little mermaid

3 Who did the people want to help?

a the prince

b the little mermaid and the prince

4 Where did the little mermaid swim to?

a She swam home to her family.

b She swam to the land.

10 Read the story. Choose the correct words and write them next to 1—4.

1	sister	father	sisters
2	how	where	when
3	there	their	where
4	brother	sisters	sister

When the little mermaid arrived back home, she told her [1] ......sisters...... that she loved the young prince. One of her sisters knew [2] .... the prince lived. "I can take you [3] ....," she said.

The little mermaid followed her [4] .... to the prince's palace.

11 Circle the correct words.

1 The magic woman of the **ocean** / **oshean** was a mermaid.

2 The magic **woman** / **women** of the ocean had a magic drink.

3 She told the little mermaid, "This will turn your **tale** / **tail** into legs."

4 "If you drink it, you will not **speek** / **speak** until the prince loves you."

5 "After you drink this, you will go **to sleep."** / **slept."**

12 **Write *can't, could,* or *couldn't.***

1 Now, the little mermaid ......could...... walk on her two new legs.

2 The little mermaid .... speak when the prince asked her a question.

3 The little mermaid .... stay in the prince's palace.

4 "...................... you speak?" the prince asked the little mermaid.

5 The little mermaid .... tell the prince that she loved him.

13 Do the crossword.

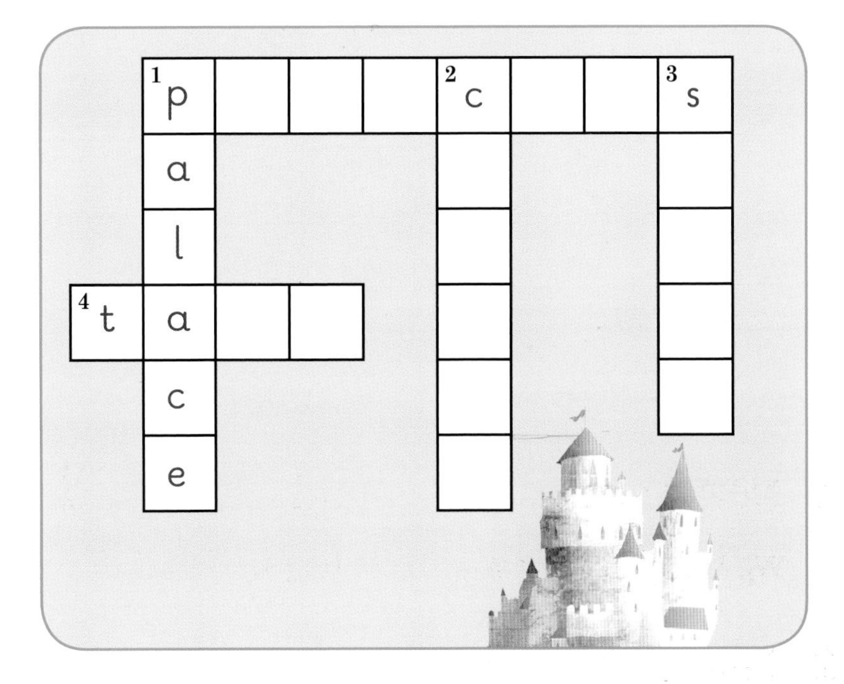

Down

1 The place where the prince lived.

2 "Can you . . . me into a person?"

3 The . . . turned the prince's ship in the water.

Across

1 A beautiful girl who came to the palace.

4 The little mermaid's . . . changed into legs.

14 Write the correct form of the verbs.

1 One day, a beautiful princess **(come)** ....came........ to the palace.

2 The little mermaid watched the prince while he **(walk)** .... with the princess.

3 They **(talk)** ...., and the prince looked happy.

4 The little mermaid **(feel)** .... very sad.

15 Read the questions. Write complete answers.

1 Can the little mermaid ever go back to her mermaid family?

No, she cannot go back to her family.

2 Do you think the little mermaid will be happy living on land? Why? / Why not?

3 What will the little mermaid miss most about her old life, do you think?

16 Order the story. Write 1—5.

.... The magic drink changed the little mermaid's tail into legs.

..1.. After the little mermaid saved the prince, she told her sisters that she loved him.

.... The prince asked the little mermaid to marry him.

.... The little mermaid's sisters told her to go to see the magic woman of the ocean.

.... The prince did not want to marry the princess.

17 Talk to a friend about mermaids.

1

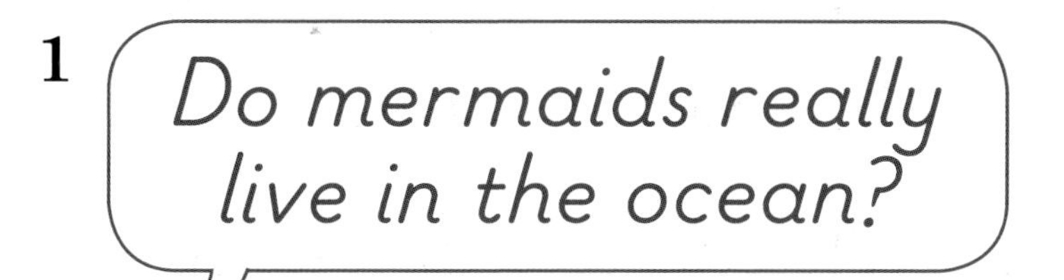

Do mermaids really live in the ocean?

No, mermaids only live in the ocean in stories!

2 Would you like to be a mermaid?

3 What do mermaids do every day, do you think?

4 What do mermaids eat, do you think?

Level 4

Ladybird Readers

Level 4

The Pied Piper of Hamelin

978–0–241–25378–6 ☐

978–0–241–25379–3 ☐

978–0–241–25380–9 ☐

978-0-241-29874-9 ☐

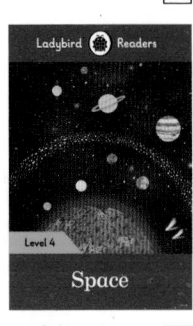

Ladybird Readers

Level 4

Space

978–0–241–25381–6 ☐

978–0–241–28430–8 ☐

978–0–241–28431–5 ☐

978-0-241-29888-6 ☐

978–0–241–28432–2 ☐

978–0–241–28433–9 ☐

978–0–241–28434–6 ☐

978-0-241-29891-6 ☐

978-0-241-29890-9 ☐

978-0-241-29889-3 ☐